SQUIRREL
AND JOHN MUIR

EMILY ARNOLD McCULLY

Farrar Straus Giroux ❖ New York

NORTH

www.fsgkidsbooks.com

Library of Congress Cataloging-in-Publication Data
McCully, Emily Arnold.
    Squirrel and John Muir / Emily Arnold McCully.
        p. cm.
    Summary: In the 1860s, a wild little girl nicknamed Squirrel meets John Muir, later
to become a famous naturalist, when he arrives at her parents' hotel in Yosemite Valley
seeking work and knowledge about the natural world.
    ISBN 0-374-33697-0
    1. Muir, John, 1838–1914—Juvenile fiction. [1. Muir, John, 1838–1914—Fiction.
2. Naturalists—Fiction. 3. Frontier and pioneer life—California—Fiction. 4. Yosemite
Valley (Calif.)—Fiction. 5. California—History—19th century—Fiction.] I. Title.

PZ7.M478415Sq 2004
[E]—dc21
                                                                                    2003045511

Love and thanks to Becky for discovering Floy

James Hutchings

Elvira Hutchings

Floy Hutchings

Cosie Hutchings

Mrs. Sproat and William Hutchings

*H*utchings' House was plain as a barn and sat in an isolated valley that lay like carpet at the foot of the mountains. It was operated by James Hutchings, his wife, Elvira, and her mother, Mrs. Sproat. The Hutchings children were Floy, her little sister, Cosie, and her baby brother, William.

Floy was the first white child born in Yosemite Valley. She tore around it like a squirrel, so that was what they called her. Papa said Yosemite Valley was the most beautiful place on earth. Floy had never been anywhere else.

Floy filled the hours by talking to the family's pet parrot, balancing on a plank
by the woodpile, making mud pies, and capturing frogs.

Papa wrote magazine articles that made people want to come and see the spectacular scenery for themselves. They made the difficult journey on horseback to stay in the hotel and go on Papa's guided tours.

Floy would barge up to the tourists and say, "Why did you come? Do snakes scare you? They don't scare me. If you get bit, I'll save you. What about bears?" Then she growled at them.

"What an odd little child," they would mutter.

Papa let Floy go on his tours. But once, when the group was too poky to suit her, she left them to follow a deer track and wasn't found until after dark.

"I can't mind you and a business at the same time!" Papa said. "You'll have to stay home from now on!"

Another time, the boys at the stable dared her to ride an unbroken horse.

"Where have you been, you wild thing!" Granny Sproat cried when she came in. "Clean yourself off before the guests see you!"

At night, Papa read Shakespeare aloud to the guests. Afterward, Floy watched them undress.

A lady heard her snickering and complained. "Mr. Hutchings, that girl of yours is a little savage!"

Papa decided that customers needed more privacy, such as would be provided by walls between their rooms. He bought a water-powered sawmill. But he couldn't run it and make the hotel improvements by himself.

One day, a man sauntered up to the hotel, as if the Fates had sent him. "I'm John Muir," he said. "I'm looking for work."

"He's just the man!" Papa cried after they had talked. "He's a sawyer, a carpenter, and an inventor!"

Floy dangled a lizard in front of the man. Tourist ladies usually squealed.

"Hello, Little Go-Quick," Muir said to the lizard. To Floy he said, "I think he wants to be free, just as we do."

Floy stared at him. She put the lizard on the ground.

"Don't pester the man," Papa said.

Papa and John Muir set up the sawmill and cut boards. John Muir built himself a small cabin, slinging his bed from the ceiling and letting a stream run right along his dirt floor.

John Muir worked hard. But he took time to wander through the valley. One day, Floy followed him along the river. He waded into the current and stretched out on a rock. After a few minutes, Floy couldn't keep quiet.

"What are you doing?" she called.

"I'm finding out how it feels to be a river rock," he said.

"Rocks don't feel," she said.

"Maybe they do. We don't know how to ask them," he said.

Floy asked, "Are you crazy?"

John Muir laughed.

Granny Sproat knew how to predict the weather. When she said it was going to snow, John Muir went dashing outside as if the house had caught fire.

"Where are you going?" Floy called.

"To listen for the sound of snowflakes landing," he said.

"I don't hear anything," Floy said.

"You're not quiet yet," Muir replied, bounding off.

When spring came and flowers bloomed in the meadows, Floy heard John Muir teasing them.

"Now, how did you come here, sweet blue-eyed darlin'?" he asked one. "Didn't I see you miles away last year?" He filled his pockets, his shirtfront, and his handkerchief with blossoms, leaves, twigs, and pebbles.

On a sultry afternoon, a thunderstorm blew up and made little Cosie cry.

"Don't be frightened," John Muir said soothingly. "Storms are nature's glory." He pulled on his jacket.

"Are you going out?" Floy asked.

"I want to hear the trees singing in the wind," he said. Floy watched him from the house as he shinnied up a tall tree and swayed back and forth like a bobolink on a reed.

"That man acts like an overgrown schoolboy," Papa said.

When he had the day off, John Muir went climbing. Floy watched him skip up sheer rock faces until he was out of sight. Hours later, he came flying back down, arms and legs churning.

"What do you do up there?" she asked him.

"I look," he said.

"Well, that's not anything," said Floy.

John Muir fell to his knees. "Look here," he said.

"It's just some old ants," Floy answered.

"Now look again," he said, handing her his little magnifying glass.

Floy gasped. A huge ant was crushing a leaf in its jaws.

"Here's another trail to follow," Muir said.

"I don't see it," said Floy.

"Grasshopper," Muir said. "Now, where is he?"

"There!" cried Floy, seeing it hop.

Floy was captivated. She used the magnifying glass to examine a bug clinging to the underside of a leaf and a dewdrop that seemed to hold the whole world.

John Muir told her the names of animals, birds, and plants, and how he listened for what they had to say.

"You've learned to see what's small and near," he said. "Now we're ready to take in the mountains."

Floy raised her eyes. "They're staring at us," she said.

"They're talking to us," Muir said.

Muir believed that the mountains and valleys had been formed by glaciers millions of years earlier. When he climbed them, he rose from ledge to ledge as if lifted by the clouds he called "sky messengers."

"I'm looking for signs of that glacier ice," he said. "They will prove that I'm right."

One day, John Muir took Floy on a walk that followed some bear tracks. He told her he had found a lookout on the north wall.

"I call it Sunnyside Bench," he said. "I sat looking long enough and eventually I saw! There are glacier trails—rocks and domes all polished by ice—from one end of the valley to the other. They show us how Yosemite Valley was formed."

"Will you take me to Sunnyside Bench?" Floy asked.

"Someday," Muir said. "When you are ready."

John Muir spent his evenings with the family, working on an article explaining his glacier theory. Then he mailed it to a New York newspaper. "Maybe they'll publish it," he said.

Papa complained. "I don't pay him to hatch crazy ideas. Scientists say there never were any glaciers here. They're calling Muir ignorant."

But pretty soon some scientists were saying Muir was right about how Yosemite Valley was formed by glaciers. A batch of tourists showed up, waving newspaper clippings and asking for the famous guide John Muir.

The ladies in the group simpered and gushed. Muir was "so handsome," "so poetic," his theory "so fascinating."

Floy thought they were silly. She expected John Muir to say he was too busy to guide them.

"Well, they are silly," he said. But he just couldn't help talking about Yosemite Valley, he loved it so much. So Floy went with him.

He explained about the glaciers and asked Floy to name the plants and animals.

"When we try to pick out anything in nature," he told the visitors, "we find it hitched to everything else in the universe."

Two ladies contrived to faint. Others whined about bee stings, torn clothes, and sore bottoms. But when they got home they spread the word about the gentle genius of the Sierras.

The more people came and asked for John Muir to be their guide instead of James Hutchings, the more Papa stewed. Finally, he couldn't stand it anymore. "Muir, you're my hired man!" he yelled. "Either that's your purpose here or you leave!"

Muir nodded. "Then I'll be on my way," he said.

Floy took off after him.

"I won't let you go!" she cried.

"There's work I must do in the world," he said.

Floy saw that he meant it. She screamed, "I hate you!" and ran off.

Muir chased after her. "Come, Squirrel. Follow me." He held out his hand.

"I'll show you Sunnyside Bench. It will be yours now."

Floy wiped her eyes.

"Everything changes, Floy. That's nature's first law."

On the way up, he sang "Highland Mary" and called out, "Squirrel, are you there?" every little while.

She called back, "Yessssss," and heard her answer trail away.

The valley lay below. It was the world, as far as Floy was concerned. Beyond, in the mist, was all the rest, where John Muir had come from and was going back to.

"Now you know the way," John Muir said. "This is where you'll have your best thoughts, I expect."

They sat for a long time. The sun sank to the horizon, and they scampered down over the rocks, as surefooted as a pair of mountain goats.

Author's Note

This story is not strictly true, but is meant to convey the spirit of what might have happened between John Muir and Floy Hutchings when they met in Yosemite in 1868. Muir did have a spot called Sunnyside Bench, but I did not depict it because I wanted a different view—one that could serve as a lookout to the valley and beyond and be a pictorial metaphor for seeing into the future and wider world.

Muir was thirty and on a quest to discover laws of nature that he himself could live by, free from society's expectations and constraints. He'd fled his father's farm in Wisconsin, been to college at Madison, worked various jobs as a mechanic/ inventor, set off on a thousand-mile walk, and arrived in Yosemite from San Francisco almost by accident.

Floy's father, James Hutchings, provided a job that sustained Muir while he used every free hour to comb the valley walls for evidence that supported his then-radical theory of glacial formation. Muir and the hotelkeeper were at ironic cross-purposes, as Hutchings's livelihood depended on attracting a tourist trade, which Muir considered at best a nuisance and at worst a threat to the wilderness. Muir wanted most of all to be left alone to explore nature and his own soul. Mrs. Jeanne C. Carr, the wife of his favorite professor at the University of Wisconsin, had made herself his champion, recognizing before anyone else his stubborn and poetical brilliance. It was she who compromised Muir's freedom by sending great men to see him and by pestering him to publish his writings. Before long, he was famous and the wider world had claimed him.

Muir spent his long life climbing mountains and urging wilderness preservation on the American government and public in his books and articles. He was the first to oppose the Westward Expansionist movement's thrust to occupy the wilderness and make it useful. His advocacy helped create Yosemite National Park in 1890 from the much smaller state park of 1864. He also founded the Sierra Club.

Yosemite was Muir's greatest stage and Floy's home—she had spent one winter in San Francisco. At only six, Floy was already a fierce, outspoken tomboy, determined never to grow up if it meant being a lady. Muir called her "that tameless one" and "a little black-eyed witch of a girl," but he took pity on her, gently instructing her in the ways of nature as he saw them. His sweetness and high spirits broke through her glowering loneliness.

Floy carried her defiant ways into adolescence, flaunting flamboyance, fearlessness, and profanity. Almost as if she were the heroine of a tragedy, she was spared ever having to move outside the park, or even growing up. She died at seventeen on a climb, struck down by a falling boulder.

Bibliography

Cohen, Michael. *The Pathless Way*. Madison: University of Wisconsin Press, 1984.

Ehrlich, Gretel. *John Muir, Nature's Visionary*. Washington, D.C.: National Geographic Society, 2000.

Muir, John. *My First Summer in the Sierra*. Boston: Houghton Mifflin, 1911.

———. *The Story of My Boyhood and Youth*. Madison: University of Wisconsin Press, 1965 (reprint).

Sargent, Shirley. *John Muir in Yosemite*. Yosemite, Calif.: Flying Spur, 1971.

———. *Pioneers in Petticoats*. Yosemite, Calif.: Flying Spur, 1966.

Stetson, Lee. *The Wild Muir*. Yosemite, Calif.: Yosemite Association, 1994.

Turner, Frederick. *Rediscovering America*. New York: Viking, 1985.

Wolfe, L. Marsh. *Son of the Wilderness*. Madison: University of Wisconsin Press, 1978 (reprint).